"Why Should I?"
Asks Jeremy

by Pamela Richards Venti
illustrated by
John Spiers

Published by The Dandelion House
A Division of The Child's World

for distribution by **VICTOR**

BOOKS a division of SP Publications, Inc.
WHEATON. ILLINOIS 60187

Offices also in
Whitby, Ontario, Canada
Amersham-on-the-Hill, Bucks, England

Published by The Dandelion House, A Division of The Child's World, Inc.
© 1983 SP Publications, Inc. All rights reserved. Printed in U.S.A.

A Book for Early Readers.

Library of Congress Cataloging in Publication Data

Venti, Pamela Richards.
  "Why should I?"

  Summary: Jeremy is very unhappy about having so many
rules to obey until he wakes up one morning to find
that all the rules are gone.
  [1. Obedience—Fiction] I. Spiers, John, ill.
II. Title.
PZ7.V563Wh 1983   [E]   83-7360
ISBN 0-89693-213-3

   1 2 3 4 5 6 7 8 9 10 11 12 R 90 89 88 87 86 85 84 83

"Why Should I?"
Asks Jeremy

*"The one who obeys me
is the one who loves me."*
—John 14:21 (TLB)

Jeremy sat at his desk. "Tap, tap, tap" we̶ his pencil.

"Jeremy!" said Mrs. Jackson. "You know the rule. Stop making that noise."

Jeremy put the pencil down. He hadn't meant
to make noise. It just happened. He looked at
the clock. Would that bell never ring?

At last, the bell did ring. The children began
to whisper.

"Quiet, children," said Mrs. Jackson. "You
know the rules." The class became quiet.

"Make two lines at the door," Mrs. Jackson said. "Now, let's go quietly through the hall."

Two by two, the children walked down the hall.

Jeremy looked up to see Mr. Miller, the principal.

Just then, Brian pulled at Jeremy's hood. Jeremy turned and frowned. Brian laughed. So Jeremy pushed him!

"Boys!" said Mr. Miller. "You know the rules. Don't push. Don't fight."

He took hold of Jeremy and Brian. He marched them all the way to the front door.

"Now," he said. "Try to remember."

"We will," they said.

9

Jeremy had to wait at the corner. The crossing guard was letting the cars go by.

Jeremy looked at the traffic signs. They were everywhere!

"Stop!" said one.

"School Crossing," said another.

"Watch for Children," said a third.

"Even the signs are rules," said Jeremy.

At last, Jeremy got home.

"Now, maybe I can do what I want," he thought. He put his lunch pail on the table. He put his jacket on the chair.

"Jeremy," said his mother. "Where does your lunch pail go?"

"In the kitchen," said Jeremy.

"That's right. And what about your jacket?"

Jeremy sighed. He put the lunch pail in the kitchen. He hung up his jacket.

Jeremy started outside to play.

"Jeremy," said his mother. "You haven't changed your clothes."

"Do I have to right now?" Jeremy asked.

"Yes, Jeremy, right now. And don't forget to feed Daisy."

Even after dinner, Jeremy had to obey.

"Take a bath!"

"Brush your teeth!"

"Put on your pajamas!"

"Let's say our prayers!"

"Go to sleep now."

Jeremy's mother tucked him in. She kissed him goodnight. She turned out the light.

"Why should I have to go to bed?" Jeremy thought. "Why are there so many rules?"

Jeremy yawned and stretched. Soon he was sound asleep.

"Time to get up," said a voice.

He was so sleepy! But Jeremy rolled out of bed. He got ready for school.

His mother fixed orange juice, toast, and oatmeal for breakfast.

"I don't want anything to eat," said Jeremy.

"Fine," said his mother. "You don't have to eat."

"I don't?" said Jeremy.

Jeremy left for school. He turned the corner. Then he blinked! There came a big bus. But it was backing down the street! The driver didn't look. He drove up on the sidewalk. He almost hit Jeremy.

"Hey!" Jeremy yelled. "You're not supposed to drive on the sidewalk!"

"Why not?" called the driver. "I like the side-walk."

By the time Jeremy got to school, he was feeling hungry. His stomach was growling. He wished he had eaten the oatmeal.

When the bell rang for lunch, instead of lining up to go outside, everyone just dashed out the door. Several children were knocked down. Jeremy was one of them.

"Why don't you make us line up?" asked Jeremy.

"Oh, we aren't going to have rules in my class anymore," said Mrs. Jackson.

The afternoon passed quickly. On the way home from school, Jeremy went by the fire station.

He saw a firefighter, winding spaghetti around the fire-hose spool!

"You're supposed to wind the fire hose," said Jeremy. "Spaghetti won't put out a fire."

"I like spaghetti," said the firefighter. "And I can do what I want."

Jeremy left, feeling funny.

When Jeremy got home, his mother asked,
"Want some ice cream?"

"Sure," said Jeremy.

"Have as much as you want," said his
mother. "Eat the whole carton if you want."

Jeremy did. It was wonderful.

And then Jeremy felt very sick.

When Jeremy felt better, he went to his friend's house in the next block.

"Let's play tag," he said to his friends.

"Okay, you're it!" yelled one.

Jeremy tagged another boy. "Now you're it!"

"No, I'm not!" said the boy.

"Yes, you are. I tagged you," said Jeremy.

"But I'm not going to be it," yelled the boy.

"Then I'm not playing with you," said
Jeremy. "You don't play by the rules. That's no
fun."

Jeremy walked out of the yard and started home.

"Look out!" someone yelled.

Dogs! Three of them came running--right at Jeremy! He jumped out of the way.

"Where did those dogs come from?" wondered Jeremy. "Why aren't they on leashes?"

"What's going on?" Jeremy asked.

And then he knew: *The rules were all gone.*

Jeremy stood all alone. He looked around. It was dark. He was cold. And scared. He shivered.

Then he felt someone touch him. It was . . .
his mother!

Jeremy looked around. He was in bed.

Outside, there were cars—on the streets.
There were dogs—on leashes. There was
peace and quiet.

Jeremy had been dreaming!

"Hurry now," his mother was saying. "Breakfast is ready.   And you don't want to be late for school."

Jeremy jumped out of bed. He felt like jumping around the room." It was a dream! It was a dream!" he said to himself.

Then Jeremy called to his mother. "No, Mom, I don't want to be late. *That's against the rules.*"

"Obey . . . for two reasons: first, to keep from being punished, and second, just because you know you should."
—Romans 13:5 (TLB)